To all the children of the known and unknown Universe

This is a New York Review Book
Published by the New York Review of Books
435 Hudson Street, New York, NY 10014
www.nyrb.com

Published for the first time in USA in 1973 by Ginn and Company – A Xerox Education Company
© 2019 RI RAUM Italic Bücher, Grafik und Design GmbH, Germany in collaboration with OOH-sounds, Italy
www.raumitalic.com / www.ooh-sounds.com
For the illustrations © 1973-2019 Diane and Leo Dillon
All illustrations are copyright protected and are the property of Diane and Leo Dillon
Published in agreement with Phileas Fogg Agency
www.phileasfoggagency.com

Library of Congress Cataloging-in-Publication Data
Names: Cain, Linda C., author. | Rosenbaum, Susan, author. | Dillon, Diane, illustrator. | Dillon, Leo, illustrator.
Title: Blast off / by Linda C. Cain and Susan Rosenbaum ; illustrated by Diane and Leo Dillon.
Description: New York : New York Review Books, [2021] | Series: New York Review children's collection | Originally published in Lexington, Massachusetts, in 1973 by Ginn and Co. | Audience: Ages 4–8. | Audience: Grades K–1. | Summary: When her friends tease her for dreaming of being an astronaut, a young African American girl uses discarded items to make a spaceship for her interstellar journey.
Identifiers: LCCN 2020057930 (print) | LCCN 2020057931 (ebook) | ISBN 9781681375687 (cloth) | ISBN 9781681376035 (ebook)
Subjects: CYAC: Astronauts—Fiction. | Outer space—Fiction. | African Americans—Fiction.
Classification: LCC PZ7.C11945 Bl 2021 (print) | LCC PZ7.C11945 (ebook) | DDC [E]—dc23
LC record available at https://lccn.loc.gov/2020057930
LC ebook record available at https://lccn.loc.gov/2020057931

ISBN: 978-1-68137-568-7

Printed in China on acid-free paper.
10 9 8 7 6 5 4 3 2 1

BLAST OFF

by **LINDA C. CAIN** and **SUSAN ROSENBAUM**
illustrated by **LEO** and **DIANE DILLON**

The New York Review Children's Collection
New York

For as long as she could remember, Regina Williams wanted to become an astronaut.

She dreamed about it. She talked about it. And she drew pictures of astronauts anywhere and everywhere.

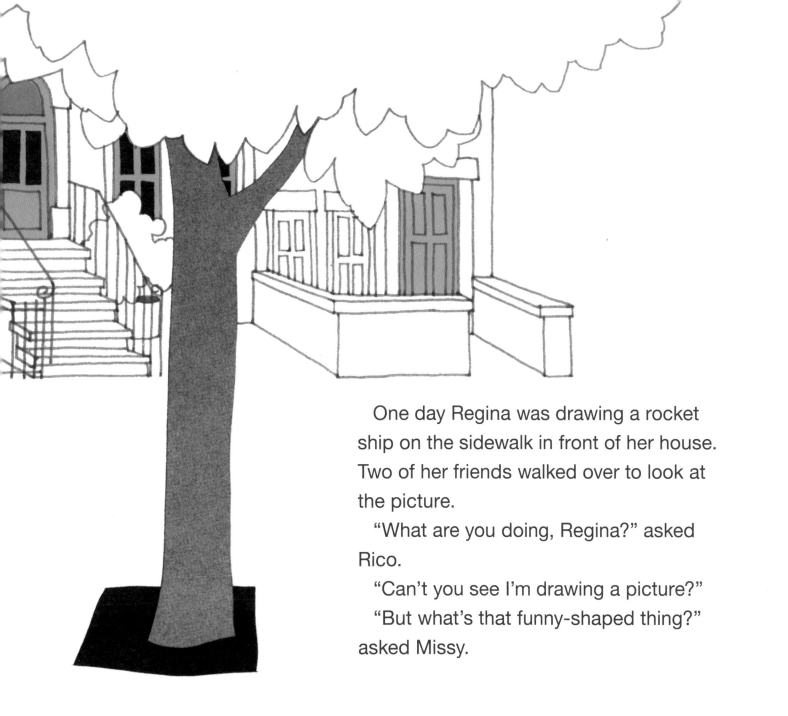

One day Regina was drawing a rocket ship on the sidewalk in front of her house. Two of her friends walked over to look at the picture.

"What are you doing, Regina?" asked Rico.

"Can't you see I'm drawing a picture?"

"But what's that funny-shaped thing?" asked Missy.

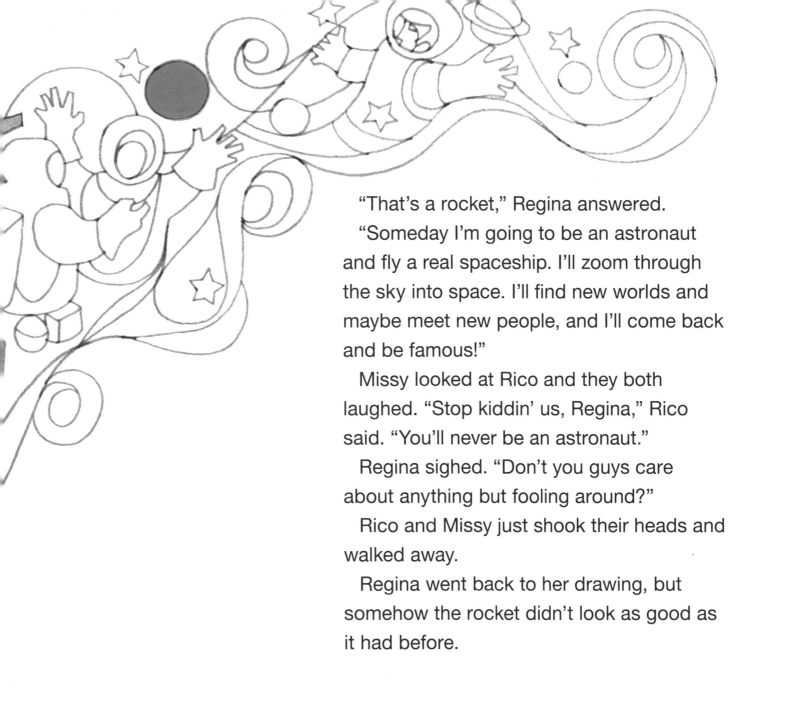

"That's a rocket," Regina answered.

"Someday I'm going to be an astronaut and fly a real spaceship. I'll zoom through the sky into space. I'll find new worlds and maybe meet new people, and I'll come back and be famous!"

Missy looked at Rico and they both laughed. "Stop kiddin' us, Regina," Rico said. "You'll never be an astronaut."

Regina sighed. "Don't you guys care about anything but fooling around?"

Rico and Missy just shook their heads and walked away.

Regina went back to her drawing, but somehow the rocket didn't look as good as it had before.

She walked up the street to the empty lot and found some pipes, boxes, cans, and an old tire.

"Wow," she thought. "This stuff will make a great spaceship."

Regina piled a few boxes on top of each other. Then she took an old trash can that had been mashed in by the street cleaners.

"This will be my space capsule," she said.

Regina began to get excited as she worked on her spaceship. She worked very hard.

Would her dream of being an astronaut really come true?

At last the spaceship was ready for blast-off. Regina sat down in the seat. It felt great to be at the controls of her spaceship. She checked the controls and the countdown began.

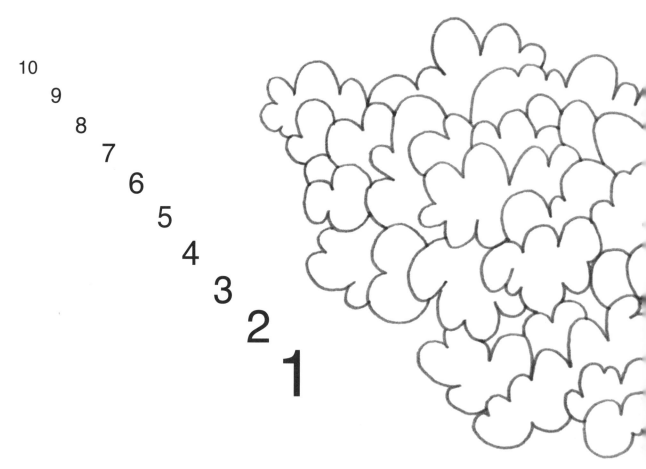

10
9
8
7
6
5
4
3
2
1

All of a sudden, Regina could feel the ship shaking around her.

"My ship is moving!" she yelled. "I'm leaving the ground!"

Regina sat frozen in her seat.

"It's really true. I'm moving through the sky—into space!"

As Regina looked through a hole in the capsule, her eyes grew wide in wonder. She saw the blue-green earth below her.

"Wow! I never would have guessed that the earth was so small."

The blackness of space was dotted with stars.

"Look at all those stars," Regina said. "There are so many of them. What's that thing coming at me? I'll bet it's a weather station. It can tell the weather way ahead of time. I wonder what all those other things are floating in space."

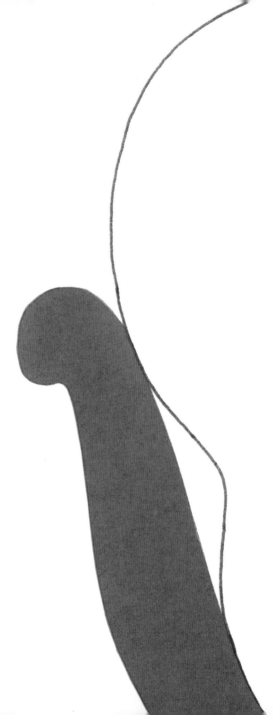

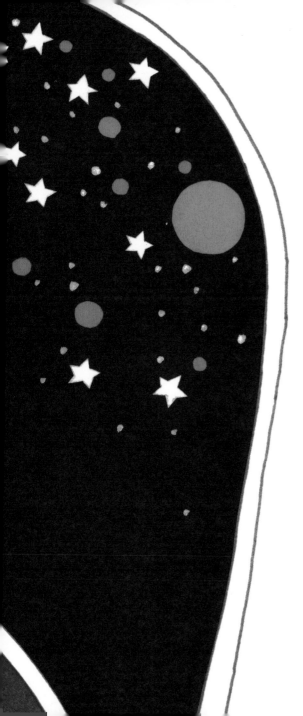

Regina leaned back in her seat and began to get a funny feeling in her stomach—the kind that comes from being alone.

It looked as if the blackness of space would never end.

"It's getting so lonely up here," she said quietly.

BANG

"What was that?" yelled Regina. "It shook the whole ship. It must have been a meteor or something."

BAM

"Help! My ship is being hit from all sides!
It feels like it's falling apart. . . ."

CRASH

All of a sudden everything was quiet again.

Regina opened her eyes and slowly crawled out of the spaceship.

Rico and Missy ran up to her. "Where have you been, Regina? We've been looking for you."

"I just went on a trip into outer space," Regina said proudly.

"Ha! The only trip you ever took was off this pile of junk," Rico said.

"No. I *was* in outer space. I saw a weather station and some meteors banged into me."

Rico and Missy just looked at each other. "Aw, come on. You were just dreaming," Rico said, laughing.

Regina didn't say anything. She just looked at them with a knowing smile.

Blast Off was written by Linda C. Cain and Susan Rosenbaum, and illustrated by Leo and Diane Dillon, who worked together on more than fifty children's books and were awarded the Lifetime Achievement Award by the Society of Illustrators in 2008.